DISNEY'S

THE LITTLE MERMAID

ALANA'S SECRET FRIEND

by Jess Christopher

DISNEY PRESS

NEW YORK

For Dr. Bob, Philosomer

Look for all the books in this series:

#1 GREEN-EYED PEARL
#2 NEFAZIA VISITS THE PALACE
#3 REFLECTIONS OF ARSULU
#4 THE SAME OLD SONG
#5 ARISTA'S NEW BOYFRIEND
#6 ARIEL THE SPY
#7 KING TRITON, BEWARE!
#8 THE HAUNTED PALACE
#9 THE PRACTICAL-JOKE WAR
#10 THE BOYFRIEND MIX-UP
#11 THE DOLPHINS OF CORAL COVE
#12 ALANA'S SECRET FRIEND

Drawings by Philo Barnhart
Cover painting by Fred Marvin
Inking by Russell Spina, Jr.

ISBN: 0-7868-4002-1

"I'm not sitting next to Adella," said Andrina, one of King Triton's seven mermaid daughters. "She snores."

"I do not!" Adella replied, seating herself on one of the coral chairs in the main lecture hall of the Museum of Natural Seastory. She lifted her chin haughtily. "My nose is much too perfect to snore."

"Perfect as a trumpet!" teased Andrina.

"Enough with the arguing," Aquata, the oldest mermaid sister, scolded them. She looked around the hall. Bright banners floated everywhere—

SAVE THE JELLYFISH! SEA FOREVER! PROTECT THE PLANKTON! Crowds of merpeople and other sea creatures were pouring into the hall through the large double doors on either side. Adella, Attina, Andrina, Arista, and Aquata were seated at one end of the second row. The other rows were filling up quickly. "Where's Ariel?" Aquata asked.

Adella shrugged. "You know Ariel. She's always late." She nudged the sister next to her. "Attina, have you seen Ariel?"

Attina looked up from the book she was reading. "What?"

The others laughed. "Can't you stop reading for one second, Attina?" Arista teased. Attina loved reading more than anything.

"This book is by Dr. Puffer," Attina explained. "I wanted to finish it before he begins his lecture." Dr. Puffer was the curator of the museum. He was about to give the opening lecture of Oceanvironmental Week, which was a new festival that King Triton had declared this year. All week long, distinguished guests from all the seven seas would be gathering at the museum and the palace to hear lectures and see displays about ways to appreciate and conserve their beautiful undersea world. King

Triton was hosting parties and formal dinners to celebrate the event, and all the merchildren of the kingdom had been given a weeklong holiday from school.

"I'm glad somebody is interested in Puffer's lecture," Andrina grumbled. "Because I know I'm not. I'm only here because Father insisted we come."

"Not interested?" Attina repeated in disbelief. "How could you not be interested in Dr. Puffer's work? It affects all of us! He's one of the most respected naturalists and oceanvironmentalists in the seven seas."

Andrina shrugged. "If it's so fascinating, why isn't Father coming himself? I'm sure the servants could have handled the last-minute preparations for the party without his personal supervision." She pretended to yawn. "All I know is I'm looking forward to a good nap."

"Never mind that," Aquata interrupted impatiently. "In case you haven't noticed, Ariel isn't the only one missing. Alana isn't here yet, either."

"Really?" said Arista. "That's strange. I know she was looking forward to this lecture. You know how she is about sea life."

"I know," said Aquata. She began to say

something else, but she was distracted by the sight of someone rushing into the hall in a flurry of fins and red hair.

"Hi, everyone!" exclaimed Ariel, the youngest of the mermaid sisters, taking a seat next to Adella at the end of the row. "Did I miss anything?"

Aquata frowned. "You're late."

"True," Ariel agreed with a grin. "But I'm early for me." Ariel liked to take long swims with her best friend, Flounder, in search of human treasures. She often lost track of time— in fact, sometimes it seemed as though she was late for things more often than she was on time.

"Have you seen Alana?" Aquata asked.

"Alana?" Ariel repeated. "Isn't she here yet? I thought she was dying to hear this lecture."

But there was no time for further discussion. Dr. Puffer had just taken the stage. He was accompanied by Sebastian, King Triton's royal court composer and the princesses' music teacher. Dr. Puffer and Sebastian had been friends for many years. The mermaids listened politely with everyone else as Sebastian introduced his old friend. Then the audience applauded as Dr. Puffer swam up to the podium.

"Good afternoon, everyone," Dr. Puffer began.

He was growing larger and more prickly by the moment. Whenever Dr. Puffer got nervous, he gulped water. Apparently he was very nervous at that moment. There were a great many important people gathered in the audience. For instance, right in the middle of the front row, Countess Oystera was sitting with her husband, Count Halfshell, and their daughter, Pearl. The count was as thin and quiet as his wife was wide and loud. The countess had donated lots of money to the museum over the years. There was even a wing named after her—the Oystera Wing for Mysteries of the Sea.

Dr. Puffer was a leading expert on mysteries of the sea—he loved to study everything from mythical creatures such as the frightening sea serpent and the fascinating humfish to legendary places such as the Bottomless Valley and the Sea of Meramera. In fact, the fabled Sea of Meramera was a particular specialty of Dr. Puffer's, and Countess Oystera's donations through the years had made it possible for the scientist to create the largest exhibit on the distant sea in any museum in all the oceans.

Nobody in the kingdom—not even King Triton or Dr. Puffer—had ever been to the Sea of Meramera. But many years ago, when

Puffer was just a small fish, a traveling merman had passed through the kingdom, claiming to have just come from Meramera. In exchange for food, the traveler had left the people of the kingdom some objects that he said came from Meramera. And he had told stories to anyone who would listen about the marvelous and mysterious creatures that lived there. The young Puffer had been fascinated. After he grew up and became curator of the museum, Dr. Puffer collected all the Meramera objects the traveler had left behind and included them in the Meramera exhibit in the museum.

Dr. Puffer was giving numerous lectures on all sorts of topics throughout Oceanvironmental Week, but for this first one he had chosen to talk about UFOs—Unidentified Floating Objects. As he began to discuss some well-known mythical UFOs—sea serpents, water nymphs, humfish, and others—Ariel's thoughts began to drift. She couldn't help wondering where Alana could be. Ariel had noticed that Alana had seemed even quieter than usual lately. She had been late to dinner three nights in a row, which was unlike her. And it was even more unlike her that she still hadn't shown up for the lecture. Alana loved to care for and learn about the creatures of the sea. She spent more time at the museum than all the other princesses put together. Where could she be?

Just then Ariel felt Adella's head droop against her shoulder. She glanced over and saw that Adella was fast asleep and snoring lightly. The other mermaids seemed to be listening closely to the lecture. This is my chance, Ariel thought. I'll just slip out and see if I can find Alana.

Gently she pushed Adella's head away and swam quietly out the end of the aisle and toward the door.

"Where are you going, Ariel?"

"Flounder! Where did you come from?" Ariel said, smiling at her best friend.

"I saw you leave the hall," Flounder replied. "I know you're up to something."

"Well, you're right," Ariel said. "I'm going out to look for Alana—she still hasn't shown up for the lecture. Do you want to help me?"

"Sure," Flounder said cheerfully. "I'm good at finding things. I helped you find the coral playground, didn't I?"

Ariel and Flounder had discovered the unusual

coral formation five days earlier in a deserted valley a few miles from the palace. It was a large underwater reef that had been shaped by the currents into dozens of tunnels and caves of different sizes, making it the perfect place to play tag or hide-and-seek.

Ariel laughed. "That's right, Flounder," she said. "I might never have found that place if you hadn't gotten stuck in one of the tunnels!"

Flounder smiled. "I won't try swimming through that skinny one again. But it's still my favorite place to play."

"I know," Ariel said. "Now all we have to do is think of Alana's favorite place."

"Could she be in the palace gardens?"

Ariel shook her head. "I don't think so. The servants are setting up all kinds of tables and things out there for the garden party Daddy is hosting today after Dr. Puffer's lecture." Ariel thought for a second. "Let's try Plankton Forest. She spends a lot of time there."

Plankton Forest was a large forest of sea plants that began about a mile from the palace. It was made up mostly of thick, tall strands of sea kelp. Narrow paths wound their way along the ocean floor, through the dark and tangled plants. Higher up in the topmost leaves there was more light. That section was rich with plankton, which had given the forest its name. Whales and fish came from all around to feed on the plankton and the plants. Alana liked to visit the forest because of the variety of sea life she could observe there.

As Ariel and Flounder swam toward Plankton Forest, they talked about Oceanvironmental Week. "I can't wait for the big concert," Ariel said. "Sebastian has been driving us crazy rehearsing 'Shimmering Sea' over and over again, but I think it will be worth it."

"You have a solo, don't you?" Flounder asked. All the princesses had beautiful singing voices, but Ariel had the loveliest one of all.

She nodded. "But that's not why I love the song," she explained. "Sebastian composed it especially for Oceanvironmental Week. The melody is a little dull, but the words are wonderful. They describe all the creatures of the sea, from crabs to starfish to eels to sharks."

Flounder shuddered. "Ugh. I think I'd like it better without the shar—What's that?" he interrupted himself.

Ariel looked ahead. They had just come over a ridge, and now Plankton Forest was spread out before them, sloping along the ocean floor as far as the eye could see. But a strange musical humming was coming from the section of the forest closest to them, and the grasses and plants were glowing with a bright yellow light. As Ariel and Flounder watched in amazement, the humming changed pitch and the light turned to bright red, then brilliant blue.

"Something weird is going on down there," Flounder said, his voice trembling. "Let's get out of here, Ariel."

Ariel swam a little closer, ignoring her friend. "Alana, are you in there?" she called.

Suddenly the humming stopped. The strange light faded.

"Come on, Ariel! Let's go!" Flounder pleaded.

"Don't be such a guppy," she replied. "It was just some lights and sounds. What's scary about that?" She swam into the forest.

Flounder followed reluctantly. "I don't like this," he muttered anxiously. "Not one bit!"

"Alana?" Ariel called again, swimming along a dark, twisting path.

Alana's voice came back to her softly. "Don't be afraid. Everything will be all right."

"I'm not afraid," Ariel answered cheerfully, swimming quickly toward her sister's voice.

As she rounded a bend in the path, she heard Alana laugh. "I wasn't talking to *you,* Ariel."

Then Ariel saw her sister. Alana's dark hair was tangled with seaweed, and her face was smudged with dirt. But her eyes were as bright as the human coins in Ariel's secret grotto.

"Isn't he beautiful?" Alana said softly.

That was when Ariel saw the fish hovering timidly behind Alana. She swam closer to look at him. He was a little smaller than Flounder and a dull silver in color. But here and there his scales winked with flashes of color. He didn't look like any fish Ariel had ever seen before.

"What is he?" she asked curiously.

"A humfish," Alana replied.

"A humfish!" Ariel exclaimed.

"A humfish!" Flounder repeated in wonder.

The silver fish moved closer to Alana. She stroked his smooth scales and smiled at him.

"I thought there was no such thing as a humfish," Ariel said. "I mean, I know Dr. Puffer has a model of one in the Mysteries of the Sea wing, but I thought he just made it up from the legends." She tried to remember what the model looked like. It was part of the exhibit on the Sea of Meramera. She wished she had paid more attention on her trips to the museum.

"This is my sister Ariel," Alana told the humfish. "That's Flounder hiding behind her. They won't hurt you, Hummer, I promise. Now show them what you can do, OK?"

The fish trembled a little. Then he hummed a note, a perfect C. As he did, his scales deepened in color to a shimmering blue. He hummed a higher note and turned green. As he continued up the musical scale, his scales went from yellow to orange to red to purple. By this time his eyes were closed, and he seemed to have forgotten all about his audience. Up and down the scale he hummed while brilliant colors flashed and flowed along his body.

"Isn't he gorgeous?" Alana exclaimed.

"He sure is," Ariel agreed wholeheartedly.

"Does he talk?" asked Flounder, staring wide-eyed at the unusual fish.

Hummer stopped humming, and the colors faded. "Of course I can talk!" he said. But he sounded more frightened than insulted.

"Where did you come from, Hummer?" Ariel asked.

"The Trembling Sea," he replied. "But the volcano there erupted, so I left. Now I'm on my way to the Sea of Meramera."

"He got here three days ago," Alana explained.

She leaned over and gave him a hug. "I've been coming here every day to see him. Right, Hummer?"

"Right, Al!" Hummer agreed.

Ariel smiled at the nickname for her sister. "What about your family?" she asked Hummer.

"I have no family. I never had one. I've never seen another fish like myself, ever. But I heard there may be other humfish in the Sea of Meramera. It sounds like such a wonderful place! I'm going to try to find it as soon as I can swim long distances again."

"He was injured when the volcano erupted," Alana told her sister. She gave Hummer another hug. "He was lucky to escape at all."

Ariel saw that Hummer's tail fin had been torn. "It looks like it's healing already," she observed.

"It's almost better," he said. "I just have to get a little stronger. I should be ready to go soon—maybe even tomorrow or the next day."

Alana shook her head worriedly. "I don't know about that," she said. She turned to Ariel. "I've been bringing him medicine and food, but the currents run awfully cold out here."

"He should come home with us," Ariel said. "Then he'll be better in no time."

Alana looked even more worried. "We've talked about that," she said slowly, glancing at Hummer. "But I don't think we should let too many people see Hummer. After all, hardly anyone believes that humfish really exist. I'm sure a lot of people would be eager to see him and maybe study him if they knew he existed."

Hummer shuddered. "They might try to keep me here and not let me go on to Meramera when I'm better," he said. "Besides, I've never lived inside before. I'd be afraid of breaking everything."

"Don't worry about that," Ariel said. "We'd help you." She turned to Alana. "I really think it would be better for Hummer to come inside to heal. He'd be much safer there."

"I don't need to," Hummer insisted, swimming even closer to Alana. "Al has been taking good care of me. I told you, I'm almost better."

Alana looked from Hummer to Ariel and then back again. "Maybe Ariel is right, Hummer," she said finally. "You *would* heal faster inside, where it's warmer."

Hummer gazed at her uncertainly, trembling a little. "Do you really think so, Al?"

"Yes," Alana said. "You'll be safer inside, too.

I worry about you staying out here alone at night, especially since you're hurt."

"You could try staying with us for just one night, Hummer," Ariel suggested. "Nobody would even have to know you were there."

"That's right," Alana said. "I can hide you in my room. We won't even tell Father."

Ariel nodded. "He'll be so busy with all the Oceanvironmental Week events that he won't notice a thing."

Alana gasped. "Oceanvironmental Week! I completely forgot about Dr. Puffer's lecture! Did I miss it?"

"You sure did," Ariel said. "Why do you think I came looking for you? Aquata and the others couldn't believe it when you didn't show up."

"Oh no," Alana said sadly. "I was really looking forward to that lecture."

Hummer looked up into her face. "Did I make you miss something, Al?" he asked. "I'm sorry!"

Alana shook her head and gave him a little smile. "That's OK, Hummer. It wasn't your fault. Besides, I'd much rather spend the time with you." She grabbed one of his fins. "Now come on, let's get you back to the palace."

Ariel peered carefully over the high coral wall around the palace garden. "It doesn't look as though we were missed," she reported to Alana, who was waiting out of sight with Hummer and Flounder. "The party is in full swing." The garden was crowded with guests who had been at the lecture. Ariel could see Countess Oystera and Count Halfshell near the palace doors. The countess was waving and calling to everyone she knew. Ariel was relieved to see that her spoiled daughter, Pearl, wasn't with her. She noticed the other princesses gathered in one corner of the garden talking to some friends from school. The King's servants were darting around, serving drinks and setting out the food for lunch.

"Good," Alana said. "I guess Aquata didn't want to worry Father by telling him we weren't at the lecture."

Ariel floated back down to join them. "I'm sure she'll be on the lookout for us, though," she said. "We'll have to find a really good way to sneak Hummer in."

Alana looked at the little silver fish thoughtfully. "It's too bad we don't have anything to make some fake fins with," she commented. "In costume I bet he could pass for an angelfish if people didn't look too closely."

"I hope you won't get in trouble for sneaking me in like this," Hummer said worriedly.

Alana gave him a pat. "We won't get in trouble, even if we do get caught," she assured him. "We just don't want anyone giving *you* any trouble."

A cheer arose from the other side of the wall, and Ariel swam up to see what was happening. "Daddy just arrived," she called down to Alana. She giggled. "And Countess Oystera has already latched on to him."

Alana giggled, too. The countess liked to tell everyone that the King was her dear, personal friend. But Triton's daughters knew better. The King tried to avoid the countess as much as possible—although she made that very difficult. "For once I'm glad to see the countess," Alana whispered. "She'll keep Father busy for the next few days."

"You're probably right," Ariel agreed. "I can't believe she invited herself to stay in the palace for the whole week. After all, she lives only a couple of miles away!" She shook her head. "At least Pearl isn't coming, too."

"Thank goodness," Alana said. Pearl was about Ariel's age, and she had come to stay at the palace once before. She had acted like a selfish, spoiled brat the whole time she was there, causing all sorts of problems for everyone, especially Ariel.

"Wait," Ariel said. "Now Daddy is going back inside." She giggled again. "I guess he's already tired of the countess." She swam back down to the others. "This is our chance. We should try to sneak Hummer in while Daddy's out of sight."

"But how?" asked Flounder.

Ariel shrugged and glanced around, hoping

for an inspiration. Then she got it. "There!" she cried, pointing. "Those baskets!"

The others turned and looked where Ariel was pointing. They saw several dozen empty baskets piled haphazardly near the garden entrance. The baskets had been used to bring in the food for the party.

"Perfect," Alana declared. She swam over and picked up one of the baskets. "It's just the right size." She opened the lid. "Come on, Hummer. In you go."

Hummer started trembling. "Are you sure?" he asked. But he did as Alana said, wedging himself into the empty basket.

Alana shut the lid, then she and Ariel lifted the basket by the handle. "Let's go," Ariel said. "Flounder, you swim ahead of us and watch for Daddy."

The princesses swam swiftly through the entrance and into the courtyard, smiling and nodding at the guests who greeted them. They sped across the garden toward the side door to the palace, which led into the kitchen. From there they knew they could make it to their bedchambers without being spotted.

But just as they had almost reached the door, a group of servants swam out of it. The headwaiter fish looked at them with surprise. "Princesses!" he cried. "You shouldn't be carrying that. It is our job and our pleasure—"

"But this is for our father," Ariel said quickly. "He wanted us to bring it." The girls turned and started swimming toward the main doorway from the garden, which led into the palace ballroom.

"Princesses!" a commanding voice cried out from behind them.

"What now?" Ariel muttered. She and Alana turned to find themselves face-to-face with Countess Oystera.

"So lovely to see you again, my dears," the countess exclaimed, rushing forward to kiss them enthusiastically on both cheeks, her long pink scarf trailing behind her. "And it was lovely to see my dear old wonderful faithful friend Triton. I wonder . . ." She moved closer, lowering her booming voice to a loud whisper. "What important affair of state could have forced him to leave this marvelous party so quickly?"

You, thought Ariel, trying not to giggle.

"He's very busy these days," Alana explained politely. "Perhaps he has to go take care of some more Oceanvironmental Week preparations. I'm sure he'll be back soon."

"But I see you have something special for him," said the countess, eyeing the basket. "A tasty special treat, perhaps? Is it a surprise?"

"You might say that," Ariel replied.

"Oh, might I have a peek?" the countess begged eagerly. Without waiting for an answer, she reached forward and lifted one edge of the lid. She squinted. "I don't see anything in here," she said, moving her face closer to the basket.

Suddenly a pair of eyes met hers. The countess shrieked. Hummer, startled, shot out of the basket. But he ran right into the countess's long pink scarf and soon found himself hopelessly entangled. He swam away with it still wrapped around him, the ends trailing behind.

"Stop, thief!" the countess hollered. Everyone looked up to see a streak of pink heading for the palace door. Thinking it was some kind of joke, the guests chuckled and then returned to their conversations. All except the other princesses, that is. They were peering suspiciously at their two sisters.

Meanwhile, Ariel, Alana, and Flounder had rushed into the ballroom after Hummer. The

little fish, confused, frightened, and half blinded by the scarf, swam headlong into a wall. Then he swam through the ballroom door into the hallway and slipped around the corner. Alana called out to him, but he was too panicked to hear her.

"Oh no!" Alana gasped. "He's heading straight for Father's office!"

The two mermaids could hear their father's powerful voice coming from the room at the end of the hall. Putting on one last burst of speed, they reached out at the same time. Each caught an end of the countess's scarf, and they hauled Hummer back swiftly.

The little fish was trembling all over. He looked exhausted by his flight. "I guess I'm not as strong as I thought," he gasped. "I don't usually get tired out this quickly."

"Don't worry, Hummer," Alana assured him. "Before long you'll be strong enough to swim all the way to Meramera."

The little fish slipped under her arm, resting there as she carried him toward her room. And in her heart of hearts Alana hoped he wouldn't swim away *too* soon.

Later that day Alana waited patiently for Ariel to come back from the party. When she heard a soft knock on her bedroom door, she opened it cautiously.

Ariel squeezed through. "I brought you some sea crisps," she said. "I hope Hummer likes them. Where is he?"

She glanced around Alana's room, then laughed. "I knew that strange silver weed of yours was good for something. I can barely see him. Hi, Hummer!"

The fish swam out from the middle of Alana's

favorite potted sea plant. He hummed a little, turning a cheerful yellow. "Hi, Ariel. Hey, Al, I like it in there."

"It's a good place for you to sleep," Alana agreed. "But not a good enough place for you to hide. We have to find somewhere better. What if someone comes into the room when I'm not here?"

"Someone like whom?" asked Hummer.

"Like our other sisters," Ariel replied. She turned to Alana. "They asked a million questions when I went back to the party. I don't think they believe you have a stomachache. Luckily Daddy was too distracted by Countess Oystera even to notice you weren't there."

"Speaking of the countess, she's someone else we have to worry about," Alana said. "You know how nosy she can be. If she found Hummer here the whole palace would know before long—especially after the scarf incident."

"Are you talking about that pink whale whose fin I tore off?" Hummer exclaimed. "You mean she's staying here in the palace?"

"She's not a whale," Alana told him, smiling. "And you didn't tear her fin. It was just a scarf."

"She won't hurt you," Ariel assured him. "But

we'll all be a lot better off if she doesn't know you're here." She glanced at Alana. "We could take Hummer with us to the concert hall."

"The concert hall?" Alana let out a gasp. "Oh no! I completely forgot! We have a rehearsal this afternoon! I'll have to miss it."

"You have to go," Ariel said. "The concert is in three days."

"But we've already rehearsed so much," Alana replied. "I could sing 'Shimmering Sea' in my sleep."

Ariel shook her head. "Sebastian seemed pretty annoyed that you missed rehearsal yesterday," she said. "If you're missing again today . . ."

"I've gotten you in trouble, Al, haven't I?" Hummer exclaimed. "I knew I would. I'll leave right now."

"No!" said both girls in unison.

Alana laughed. "You don't have to worry so much, Hummer. I love having you here. I'm your friend, remember?"

"My best friend," Hummer replied shyly. He hummed softly, and his scales turned a beautiful shade of soft lilac.

Ariel picked up Alana's school bag and dumped out the books that were in it. "I think he'll fit inside this. Want to give it a try, Hummer?"

Hummer wriggled into the bag. "Very cozy," he announced.

"Good. Now come on," Ariel said to Alana. "We're going to be late."

The mermaids lifted the book bag and headed for the concert hall. The other five sisters and Octavio, the one-octopus band, were already beginning their warm-up scales when Ariel and Alana arrived.

Ariel and Alana quickly took their places, and Alana shoved her bag under her chair. Her sisters were staring at her curiously.

"Feeling better, Alana?" Andrina asked.

"Much better, thanks," Alana replied quietly.

There was no time for further questions. Sebastian rapped his baton sharply. "How nice of you two to come," he remarked dryly to Ariel and Alana. "Shall we begin?"

The sisters sang their way through the program. They had never performed better. When they had finished a sad ballad about water pollution, Sebastian wiped away a tear. "Beautiful! Beautiful!" he exclaimed. "I can see that all our extra practice is paying off. Now, Princesses, our finale."

The sisters groaned.

"Can't we do something other than 'Shimmering Sea'?" complained Andrina.

"No offense, Sebastian, but the music is a little boring," added Attina.

The others nodded. Sebastian frowned and raised his baton. "Let us begin," he said sternly. The princesses knew better than to argue when Sebastian used that tone of voice, so they just waited for his cue and started the song.

A few measures into it, they all noticed something different about the tune. It was the same song they had been practicing for weeks, but suddenly it didn't sound the same. There were new notes along with the ones Octavio was playing—a haunting harmony.

"Stop! Stop!" cried Sebastian. "Where are those notes coming from? Who is doing that harmony?"

Aquata, Andrina, Attina, Adella, and Arista looked around blankly. "We're not doing anything different, Sebastian," Arista said.

Sebastian frowned and stared down at his musical score for a moment. "All right," he said finally. "Let's try it again from the top."

They began again. For the first few bars the music sounded the same as always. Sebastian closed his eyes and smiled, swaying to the rhythm. Then that humming harmony began to weave itself into the song again. Out of the corner of her eye, Alana saw a purplish blue light glowing out from the bag beneath her chair. Arista had noticed the glowing bag, too. Her eyes grew wide, and she stopped singing. Adella turned to see what was happening and watched as the bag began to rise.

"For the love of Beethofin!" exclaimed Sebastian, his eyes flying open. "Where is that coming from?" The music stopped. The bag dropped to the floor again. "Octavio, are you playing a harmonica or something?"

The octopus shook his head, glancing over toward Alana's chair. Ariel looked at Alana in dismay.

Sebastian grumbled to himself, then raised his baton again. Again he closed his eyes, concentrating on the sound. And again the bag hummed and glowed. This time all the sisters and Octavio stared at the shimmering thing. Adella and Arista stopped singing. Ariel reached for the bag and thrust it back under the chair.

Sebastian's baton came down with a crack. "For the last time, where is that new harmony coming from?" he shouted, his eyes flying open.

"Harmony?" Ariel asked, pretending to be confused. "What harmony? Did you hear any new harmony, Alana?" She nudged her sister.

"What?" said Alana. "Oh, uh, no. No harmony at all. Sounds like the same old song to me."

"Maybe you're hearing it in your head," Ariel told Sebastian earnestly. "After all, you're a composer. All great composers hear music in their heads, don't they? Beethofin did."

"Beethofin was a *genius*," said Sebastian. Then he blinked at Ariel. "Perhaps you're right! I'm hearing it in my head. And it's wonderful! It is exquisite! Why, I must write it down before I forget it. My dear girls, wait until you hear. You'll love it!"

Sebastian rushed out of the room. When he was gone, all the sisters turned to stare at the bag. Octavio set down his instruments. He slithered past the girls toward the door but stopped and waved seven of his eight tentacles—one for each sister—in their faces. His rubbery face puckered into a smile. "Something strange is going on around here," he said, and left.

As soon as the door closed behind Octavio, the mermaids gathered around Alana's chair. Ariel gently lifted the book bag and opened the flap. Hummer swam out and stared at the princesses.

"Oh!" the sisters gasped when they saw him. His scales were a shimmering pale blue tinged with green.

Hummer swam to Alana and looked up into her face. "I just couldn't help myself, Al," he said apologetically. "With all that wonderful singing going on, I just had to hum. Are we in trouble?"

"I think we got out of it this time," she replied, smiling. "Thanks to Ariel. Hummer, these are my other sisters. They'll keep your secret—won't you?" she asked, turning to them.

"What secret is that?" Aquata asked.

With Ariel's help, Alana told them everything that had happened in the last few days. The other princesses stared at Hummer in awe.

"I can't believe I'm really looking at a humfish!" Attina exclaimed. "Especially after hearing Dr. Puffer lecture about them just this morning!"

"Dr. Puffer?" Hummer asked curiously.

"Yes," Alana explained. "He runs the museum, and he knows more than anybody about all kinds of sea creatures—even ones nobody here has ever seen before, like you."

"He knows about humfish?" Hummer asked.

Attina nodded. "He even has a model of one in the museum. It looks almost like you, except it's a little smaller and the tail is different."

"That's right," Alana said. "He also wrote a book about mythical creatures, including humfish."

"What's a book?"

"You've never seen a book before?" Arista said.

"Let's go to the library and show him,"

suggested Attina. She smiled at Hummer. "I'll read to you about the Sea of Meramera if you like."

"Oh, I'd like that very much!" Hummer exclaimed. "Thank you, Attina!" He swam after her as she left the concert hall and headed toward the palace library. The other mermaids followed.

"Be careful!" Alana called anxiously. "Don't let anyone else see you!"

But Hummer was busy talking to Attina about Meramera and didn't hear her. Luckily they didn't encounter any guests or guards along the way. When they entered the library, Hummer suddenly paled. He swam quickly to Alana's side, trembling.

"W-what's that?" he squeaked.

Alana followed his gaze to the King's new model of a shark. "Oh, that!" she said. "Don't worry, Hummer, it's not real. Dr. Puffer made that shark for our father in honor of Oceanvironmental Week. It's like the models he has in the museum. It's supposed to remind us that all creatures are an important part of the undersea world, even scary ones."

"It gives me the jellies," said Hummer.

"The jellies?" Andrina repeated. "What's that?"

"I can guess," said Arista. "Look at him, he's shaking like a jellyfish!"

Meanwhile, Attina was searching the shelves. "I just read a wonderful book about Meramera a few weeks ago," she said. "Now, where is it?" Suddenly she swished upward and grabbed a large book off the topmost shelf. "Oh, here's one."

She swam over to one of the big library tables and set the book down. The others gathered around. Hummer took a position over her shoulder so he could see.

"This isn't the exact book I was thinking of," said Attina. "But this one is pretty good, too."

"Look at that!" exclaimed Adella, pointing to the picture on the cover. It showed a landscape full of beautiful coral reefs, graceful plants, and colorful fish of all shapes and sizes. "It's gorgeous!"

"It sure is," Hummer replied in awe. He watched as Attina opened the book and began paging through it.

"Here's something about humfish," she said. " 'The mythical humfish is said to be the most beautiful of all the fish in Meramera. Its silvery scales turn all the colors of the spectrum when it makes its melodious sounds, and all the creatures in the sea love to watch and hear it sing.' "

"Oh, that sounds lovely!" said Aquata with a sigh. Hummer just smiled and let out a few tinkling notes while his scales shimmered pale pink and violet.

They were all so engrossed in the book that they didn't even hear the library door open. It wasn't until they heard Dr. Puffer's voice that they realized they were no longer alone.

"This, my friends, is the high point of our tour," he was saying to the group of merpeople following him, which included Countess Oystera and Count Halfshell.

"Tour?" Ariel gasped.

Hummer turned pale and slipped beneath the table while Attina slammed the book shut.

"Ah, good afternoon, Princesses," Dr. Puffer said, noticing them for the first time. "Please pardon the interruption. Your father has asked me to show his guests some of the marvelous plants and creatures he has here at the palace."

The sisters were speechless for a second, but then Aquata found her voice. "No problem at all, Dr. Puffer. Please carry on," she said graciously.

Dr. Puffer nodded and turned back to the tour group. "Over here you'll see a reproduction of a shark, which I created at King Triton's personal request."

Everyone swam over to take a closer look at the model—except Countess Oystera. She gave the princesses a big smile and a little wave and started swimming toward them. She had changed into a long flowing yellow gown with a matching yellow scarf around her neck. When she reached the table, she pulled out a chair to sit down. Hummer, who had been hiding there, rushed to the next chair. The countess looked down, her brow wrinkled.

Then she pulled out the next chair. Hummer darted over the side of the chair. Then Alana saw him whip around behind the countess. Then he disappeared—or so it seemed.

Alana heard a long, low, sweet humming note. She realized her friend had hummed himself as yellow as the countess's scarf.

The countess heard the music, too, somewhere behind her head. She spun to the left, then to the right, trying to figure out where it was coming from. But each time the little yellow fish was quicker.

Before long the countess was turning faster

and faster until she looked like a fish chasing its own tail. Suddenly she stopped, looking quite dizzy. "Oh my, oh my!" she gasped.

Hummer, who was just as dizzy, drifted out from the yellow scarf. Alana gave him a light push under the table. Ariel held out her arm to the countess. "Let me help you," she said sweetly.

As she led the swaying and weaving merwoman back to the tour group, she could hear her sisters giggling behind her. Ariel bit her lip to stop herself from laughing as well. If Hummer is going to be around here for long, she thought, we could be in for some real mischief!

6

Two days later Alana awakened to a crash. She sat straight up in bed. "Hummer?"

Her favorite plant was still on its shelf. But Hummer was not sleeping among its silvery fronds.

"Help," the little fish called softly.

Alana sprang out of bed. "Oh dear!"

She tried not to laugh. Hummer was in the corner of the room, completely tied up in the shell mobile Attina had given her for her last birthday. "How did you pull that out of the ceiling?" she asked.

"I was practicing," Hummer replied. "I was working on my quick turns and dodges. When your mobile spins, I swim in and out between the shells as fast as I can. But I, uh, sort of missed."

With deft fingers, Alana began to untangle the mess. One of the mobile's strings had broken. She picked up the cracked shell that had been attached to it.

"Look what I've done!" Hummer said. "Al, I'm sorry."

"It's OK, Hummer," Alana told him. "I can find another shell to replace it."

"I keep breaking things! First that vase in the library—"

"You didn't mean to," Alana tried to soothe him.

"—then Adella's mirror—"

"She'll get over it."

"It's just that when you're inside there are things everywhere," Hummer said. "All you have to do is move your tail and something's right there, waiting to be knocked over."

"You're doing fine, Hummer, really," Alana said. "We know you've never lived inside before. And we all love having you here. Everybody's been having fun." She tried to think of something to take his mind off his clumsiness. "How's your tail feeling?"

Hummer swished it back and forth. "Great!" he said happily. "I'll be able to swim to Meramera soon. Maybe tomorrow! I can't wait!"

Alana caught his tail lightly in her hand and looked at it. It seemed to be completely healed. Only a thin white scar showed where it had been ripped. "Well, tomorrow may be a little too early," she said, not liking the thought that her new friend would leave so soon. "You should rest a while yet and get your strength up."

"When I'm gone, you won't have any more trouble with me breaking things all the time," Hummer said.

"You're not causing any trouble, Hummer!"

"I'll try not to break anything else before I leave," he added.

"Hummer!"

Just then there was a knock on Alana's door. "Alana? Hummer?" came Ariel's whispered voice. "It's just us."

She opened the door and swam in, with Attina, Adella, and Flounder right behind her. Ariel smiled and held up two whispery soft fake fins and a long, silky tail.

"What's that for?" Hummer asked.

"It's for a funny-looking angelfish," Flounder teased.

"It's your disguise, Hummer," Ariel said. "Now you won't have to sneak around as much."

"That's right," said Adella. She was holding her makeup bag. "When we're through, nobody will recognize you."

"Well, not unless they're looking pretty closely," Ariel corrected her. "You'll still have to be careful."

"Oh, Hummer, we'll be able to have so much fun!" exclaimed Alana, clapping her hands. "We can go all kinds of places. There's another garden party tomorrow afternoon, and our big concert is tomorrow night. Later in the week I'll take you to the museum if you like. It'll be great!"

"I'm not sure the museum is such a good idea," Attina warned. "This costume will fool most people, but I don't think it will fool Dr. Puffer."

Alana shrugged. "Well, we'll see," she said.

Then they set to work transforming Hummer into an angelfish. They laughed as they watched him try to adopt the graceful swimming style, and he laughed right along with them. Before

43

long, extra fins and all, he was doing well enough to get by.

* * *

Later that day, when Hummer and the seven mermaid sisters returned from exploring the kingdom, Alana had a statue of King Triton under her arm. It was one of the ugliest souvenirs any of them had ever seen—especially now that one arm was broken off. Hummer had forgotten about his extra-long angelfish tail. With one quick flick he had accidentally flung the statue against the wall in a souvenir shop.

"You break it, you buy it," the store manager, a grumpy-looking snail, had said with a sniff.

So Alana had bought it. "It's OK. It's OK," she kept telling the apologetic Hummer. "I've always wanted a statue like this. It looks just like Father—"

"—on a really bad day," Andrina finished for her with a laugh.

The sisters, Hummer, and Flounder had giggled at that one all the way home.

* * *

The following afternoon at the garden party, Hummer trailed along behind Alana, gazing around. The palace garden was a maze of sea flowers. Tables were laden with platters of delicious sea fruits. Servants carried shells full of tasty foods and drinks. Everyone was waiting for King Triton to make his entrance.

Hummer was enjoying himself. Conversation swirled all around him. He had to remind himself not to hum along as Octavio performed a string quartet by Schuperch. Hummer stopped to listen to the music as Alana drifted off to talk to someone. A moment later Hummer noticed Countess Oystera sitting at a table nearby.

The large merwoman was dressed in purple from head to tail. Lying on the table next to her was the most beautiful ring of purple sea berries Hummer had ever seen. He wondered what it tasted like. Feeling brave and adventurous in his costume, he waited until the countess turned away to speak to someone, then darted in and took a bite out of the mysterious ring of berries.

He was disappointed to find it was rubbery and hard to chew. It didn't have much taste. Still, the little fish chewed on. And on. And on. At last he swallowed.

Suddenly there was a horrible shriek. "My bracelet!" screamed the countess, pointing straight at Hummer. "That fish is eating my bracelet! I just took it off for a moment!"

Hummer trembled, not sure what to do or which way to swim. He was vaguely aware that Alana and Ariel were rushing toward him. He gazed for a second at the broken purple ring. Then he took off.

"Catch him!" someone shouted. "Catch that angelfish!"

The King arrived in the garden just in time to see guards swimming every which way. Tables were overturned and sea flowers tangled as everyone tried to catch Hummer.

"BE STILL!" King Triton thundered. "BE STILL, I SAY!"

Everyone stopped immediately, turning toward the King. Everyone except Hummer. Alana saw her friend slip into the palace through the ballroom door.

Countess Oystera rushed over to the King, arms flailing. "Oh, my dear, dear King Triton! It was horrible! That awful fish ripped my beautiful bracelet off my arm and chewed it to pieces!"

The princesses were huddled nearby, listening. "He did *not* rip it off her arm!" Alana whispered indignantly to her sisters.

Aquata shook her head. "You know the countess," she said. "She loves to exaggerate."

Ariel noticed that Alana looked very worried. "Hummer will be all right," Ariel said. "He knows his way around now."

"And he's so clever at hiding," Arista added. "He'll probably just lay low until the party is over."

"I'm going to go look for him," Alana said.

"Let him be," Andrina advised. "This is good practice for Hummer. He'll be on his own soon enough."

Alana didn't want to think about that. "I'm going to go look for him," she repeated stubbornly.

The other sisters exchanged glances. "Well, you shouldn't go alone," Ariel said. "I'll come with you and help you search."

"Me, too," Attina volunteered.

Aquata looked worried. "I hope Father doesn't notice you're all gone," she said.

"Don't worry," Ariel said with a laugh. "The rest of you will just have to distract him!"

Then she, Attina, and Alana headed into the palace. Once inside, they separated. Attina went to check the kitchen and library. Ariel swam toward the girls' bedrooms. Alana decided to search the far wing of the palace, where the guests were staying.

They met up again in the main hallway. "Any sign of him?" Ariel asked the others. They both shook their heads.

"He's gone for good!" Alana wailed. "I knew it! He was so worried about breaking things and causing trouble. After this I'm sure he'll never come back!"

"There are a lot of places in the palace we haven't searched yet," Ariel reminded her.

Attina sighed. "It will take forever to look everywhere," she said. "Especially since he's so good at hiding. And if we call his name out loud everyone will start wondering who he is."

Suddenly Ariel had an idea. "What if we sang?" she suggested excitedly. "We could swim around and sing 'Shimmering Sea'! He'll recognize it and know it's us."

"What a wonderful idea!" Alana said, cheering up. "If he's anywhere in the palace, we'll definitely find him!"

Once more the sisters separated to continue their search. As she swam, Alana sang, stopped, and listened. She sang, stopped, and listened again. Each time she strained to hear the little fish's line of harmony. The song's melody seemed plain and sad now without it.

After a while she began to hear other voices singing the song. At first she thought it was just Ariel and Attina. Then she rounded a corner and saw Andrina singing in the hallway.

Andrina gave her a wink. "We told Father we had to practice some more for this evening's concert," she whispered. "And in a way, we *are* practicing!"

While the seven sisters were still singing and searching, the party began to break up. Guests floated back into the palace and heard the princesses singing. Some of them began humming or whistling along. Before long the guards and servants joined in as well.

"It's everywhere!" Sebastian cried as he entered the palace. He stopped in the hallway to listen, a frown on his face. "And they're doing it so badly! What in the name of Mozshark is going on?"

* * *

By early evening the sisters still hadn't found Hummer.

"We've done the best we can," Aquata said, giving Alana a hug. "He must have left the palace. We'll just have to wait for him to come back on his own."

Alana shook her head and pushed her sister away. "We have to search outside."

"We can't search the entire kingdom," Andrina said.

"Especially not now," Arista added. "We have

to start getting ready for our concert right after dinner."

"Besides," Attina said, "if he's outside, he's probably doing fine. After all, he's used to living outside, Alana. For him, this palace contains more trouble and danger than the whole outdoors. Remember, he escaped a volcano and made it here on his own."

"Yes, but he was injured," Alana said with a frown.

"He's healed now, Alana," Ariel said gently.

"He isn't!" Alana insisted. "He's not ready to be on his own yet!"

Ariel and the others stared at her, surprised at her tone.

"I mean, he may be healed, but he's not ready to go. Not yet!" Alana's cheeks grew pink, and her big blue eyes filled with tears. "I know him better than any of you!"

The sisters were silent for a moment, not knowing what to say. Finally, Adella broke the silence. "Well, I have to go," she announced. "I want to wash my hair before dinner so it will look its best for the concert." She swam off, and Andrina and Attina drifted away, too.

Aquata looked at Alana. "Come on, Alana," she said. "Why don't you start getting ready, too? We have a little while before we have to go to dinner."

Alana turned away and started swimming toward the door. "I'm going to look for Hummer."

"Alana!" Arista cried. "You can't! If you're not here for the concert, we'll all get in trouble!"

"Hummer is the one in trouble," Alana called back over her shoulder.

Ariel looked at Aquata and Arista helplessly. "Cover for us at dinner if you can, OK?" she said quickly. Then she began swimming after Alana. "Hold on, Alana!" she called. "I'm coming with you!"

Ariel and Alana swam quickly in the direction of Plankton Forest. Alana's face was pale and worried. "What if Hummer is sick?" she said anxiously as she and Ariel darted over a grassy ledge. "He ate that piece of bracelet. What if it poisoned him?"

"Alana, try not to think about—"

"What if he's lost somewhere?" Alana interrupted. "What if he's hidden and sick and afraid to come out?"

"Try not to imagine the worst, Alana," Ariel said. "Wait until we find out what really happened.

Hummer may be safe and sound in the forest."

"What if it were Flounder who was missing?" Alana said. "What would *you* be imagining?"

Ariel slowed down. "The worst," she admitted, and reached over to give her sister a hug.

"Where is Flounder, anyway?" Alana asked as they resumed swimming. "He could be helping us search."

Ariel thought for a moment, trying to remember the last time she'd seen Flounder. "He was at the garden party," she said slowly. "At least he was there at the beginning. But after all the excitement—" She shrugged. "I don't think I saw him after Hummer swam out." Suddenly Ariel's eyes lit up. "That's it!"

"What?"

"I have a feeling I might know where one— make that two—missing fish are!" she said, changing direction. "Follow me!"

"But Plankton Forest is the other way."

"First we have to go see Flounder's latest discovery," Ariel told her sister. A few minutes later they crested a high coral ridge, then looked down into a small sea valley. "There!" Ariel said, pointing. "The coral playground!"

Alana looked. "Wow!" she exclaimed, staring down at the unusual shapes jutting up from the valley floor. The coral formed all sorts of things—from caves large enough for three mermaids to fit into to short passageways too narrow for a small fish to swim through. "This looks like a great place to play," Alana observed as the sisters swam down into the valley.

Ariel nodded. "Flounder loves it here."

At that moment the sisters saw Flounder come darting out the end of one of the larger tunnels. He spun around, then swam into another opening.

Then Hummer popped out of the large tunnel. One torn angelfish fin still hung off his back. Before he could rush into another tunnel, Flounder emerged from one nearby. A chase began. Laughing, the two little fish darted in and out of the entrances and openings in the coral, trying to surprise each other. Hummer glowed and hummed as he swam, and the valley echoed with musical sounds.

Ariel and Alana swam swiftly to the coral. Hummer and Flounder popped out at the same time and found themselves face-to-face with the mermaids.

Hummer laughed. "Hi, Al! Hi, Ariel! Did you come to play with us?"

Alana didn't know whether to laugh or cry.

She was relieved to know that Hummer was all right. But she was angry at him, too, for causing her such worry. "We've been looking for you everywhere, Hummer!" she exclaimed.

"Well, you found me," he replied cheerfully.

"Alana was very worried about you, Hummer," Ariel said.

"Why?" asked the little fish.

"I—I didn't know where you had gone," Alana replied. "I thought you were scared and had run away. And I was afraid you might be sick or even poisoned from eating that bracelet."

"Well, I *was* scared when that countess yelled at me," Hummer admitted. "But then I ran into Flounder inside the palace."

"Bam!" Flounder said with a laugh. "He wasn't watching where he was swimming."

"Then Flounder brought me here to play," Hummer continued. "You shouldn't worry, Al. I feel great!"

Alana nodded and turned away. She didn't want him to see how she felt.

But Hummer swam around to look at her face. "You're crying! Al, don't cry!"

Alana's voice trembled as she replied. "I thought I'd never see you again. I thought you'd left without saying good-bye."

"But you're my best friend," Hummer said in surprise. "I wouldn't do that!"

Alana nodded and wiped her eyes.

"When I leave," Hummer said, "I will say good-bye first. I promise."

"Come on, Alana," Ariel said quietly. "We'd better head back. We don't want to be late for the concert." Then she turned to the fish. "Hummer, you need some repair work on that disguise. Why don't you wait until everyone has gone to the concert hall. Then Flounder can help you sneak back in and fix yourself up." She and Alana started back toward the palace.

* * *

That evening when the princesses finished the new version of "Shimmering Sea," they received a loud ovation from the audience. Sebastian was so proud that he could hardly contain himself. "What harmony!" he exclaimed as they all left the stage after taking their bows. "It was magical, my dears. Absolutely magical!"

But for Alana the most magical thing about the song was that it reminded her of Hummer. When she heard the harmony Sebastian had added, she knew she would always remember it as the humming of her beautiful little fish.

Two days later Alana awoke to shimmering pinks and golds. Her room was filled with soft humming sounds.

"I thought I'd never wake you!" Hummer said. "Good morning, Al."

"Good morning," Alana replied with a yawn. She sat up and watched her friend. He was showing off, dodging in and out of the shells in the mobile she had rehung from the ceiling. Each move was clean. "You're doing great, Hummer!"

Hummer curled his tail under and did a quick somersault. "Thanks to you, Al!"

"Are you hungry?" she asked.

The fish swam down to Alana's dresser. A breakfast tray was there. "Arista brought it," Hummer said.

"Oh! I must have really overslept," exclaimed Alana with surprise. She hadn't realized she was so tired. She and the other princesses had spent the day showing Hummer more of their favorite places in the kingdom. Then at the formal dinner party that evening Countess Oystera had talked her ear off. But now Alana felt refreshed by her good night's sleep.

"Attina is waiting for me in the library," Hummer went on. "She finally found that great Meramera book she was looking for the other day. She wants to show it to me."

"Then go ahead," Alana said. "I'll join you in a few minutes."

The little fish rushed off. Alana, humming her wake-up song, combed her hair and ate her breakfast. Then she swam to the library.

As she entered, she heard Attina reading aloud. Hummer, Flounder, and the other princesses were gathered around her, listening closely.

" 'In the Sea of Meramera,' " Attina read, " 'the currents are warm and gentle. Brightly colored fish live peacefully with one another. Some people believe these creatures feed on starseeds—' "

"Hi, Al," Hummer greeted her excitedly as she swam up to the group. "Come and listen to this! Meramera sounds so wonderful. You would love it there, Al. It sounds as though there are so many interesting fish! And this book even has a map that will help me find it!"

Alana frowned a little. "You won't need that map until you're ready to go, though, Hummer."

"I am ready," he said, doing a little flip above the mermaids' heads.

Alana bit her lip, then looked at the map. With her finger she traced the path Hummer would have to take. "You'll have to swim for days and days until you reach the Lava Sea," she said softly, "where the firefish live. Then through the Sea of Serpents, where there are monsters longer than this room. And then on to Ghost Crab Flats. Nobody from this kingdom has ever made it that far." She glanced up at Hummer. "Are you ready for that?"

He had paled as she spoke until his scales looked almost white.

"Come on, Alana," Andrina said. "What are you trying to do, scare him to death?"

"Then there's the Valley of Swallowing Sands," Alana continued grimly, looking back down at the map. "And Shark Haven. Are you sure you're ready for Shark Haven?"

"I—I think I am," Hummer replied. But he didn't sound very sure.

Alana pointed to the shark model. "Hummer, that *model* gives you the jellies. How are you going to face the real thing?"

The little fish didn't say anything.

"I just want what's best for you," Alana told him. "Promise me you won't go. Not yet."

"I promise I won't go today," said Hummer slowly. He gave her a tentative smile. "You said you'd take me to the museum today."

Alana smiled back with relief. "I'll go get your disguise."

When Alana returned with the repaired angelfish disguise, Ariel helped her attach the silky fins.

Alana whistled while she worked. She was feeling hopeful again. It will be good for Hummer to see Dr. Puffer's models, she thought. Then he'll see how large and scary some sea creatures are. He'll realize what a little fish he is—and change his mind and stay.

But Ariel was thinking about something else. She couldn't help wondering what Hummer would think of Dr. Puffer's Sea of Meramera exhibit in the Mysteries of the Sea wing. It was the most beautiful of the many beautiful exhibits at the museum. The exhibit was sure to make Hummer even more excited about leaving for Meramera than the pictures in Attina's book had. The thought made Ariel a little sad. She knew how much Hummer wanted to reach the Sea of Meramera and find other humfish—but she also knew she would miss the cheerful little fish when he was gone.

She glanced over at Alana, who was chattering excitedly to Hummer about the museum. Ariel knew that Alana had grown more and more attached to Hummer ever since his arrival in the kingdom. As much as Ariel was going to miss Hummer herself, she knew that Alana would miss him a whole lot more.

* * *

When Alana and Hummer arrived at the museum, it was almost completely deserted. It was the last day of Oceanvironmental Week, and many of King Triton's guests were leaving.

Still, Alana thought Hummer seemed a little anxious.

"What is it?" she asked as they swam down the Hall of Sharks. "Do the exhibits really frighten you?"

"It's not the exhibits," Hummer confessed. He glanced around and gulped. "Although they are pretty scary. But what really makes me nervous is that we might run into Dr. Puffer."

"Dr. Puffer? But he loves all kinds of sea creatures," Alana said. "You don't need to be scared of him. He's dedicated his life to teaching others about the wonders of our sea."

"But what if he wants to teach others about me? What if he wants to turn *me* into an exhibit?" Hummer asked.

"Is that what's worrying you?" Alana asked. "Dr. Puffer never uses live creatures in the museum. These are all just models."

Still, Hummer's words made Alana think. What *would* Dr. Puffer do if he saw Hummer? Maybe he would want to keep him here in the kingdom to study him. Alana glanced at her friend and then shuddered. As much as she would love for Hummer to stay in the kingdom forever, she hated the thought of him being held against his will. She decided she'd better keep a sharp lookout for the scientist until they were safely out of the museum.

After the Hall of Sharks, Alana led the way to the sponge and coral wing. Hummer loved the beautiful colors of the exhibits there. He even hummed himself to match some of his favorite pieces.

Next they went to see the jellyfish exhibit. Then Hummer wanted to visit the crustacean wing. "I want to learn about creatures like Sebastian," he told her eagerly. "I do love his music!" He began humming "Shimmering Sea," his scales glowing blue and gold.

Alana smiled at his interest. "Sebastian has given Dr. Puffer a lot of help with this wing," she told her friend when they reached the crustacean wing. "They've been friends practically forever." She pointed to a model of a crab for which Sebastian had posed. "See? There he is."

"No. *There* he is," Hummer said with a loud gulp, pointing in the opposite direction.

Alana spun around. Coming down the hall, waving a claw, was Sebastian. And right behind him was Dr. Puffer!

"Princess Alana! My very favorite daughter of King Triton! A student of the sea like myself! How perfectly marvelous to see you again!" Dr. Puffer exclaimed, rushing toward Alana with a broad smile.

"Hello," Alana said. She glanced at Hummer, hoping his extra fins were in place.

Both Sebastian and Dr. Puffer turned to greet Alana's friend.

"I don't believe we've met, young fish," Sebastian said politely.

Hummer edged behind Alana.

"This is—er—Humble," she said quickly. "He's very shy."

"He's very unusual," Dr. Puffer observed, moving closer for a better look. "I don't believe I've ever seen an angelfish quite like him."

"I have," Sebastian murmured slowly. "In the garden yesterday."

Dr. Puffer swam in a circle around Hummer. "How curious," he said. "How perfectly curious!"

Under the scientist's sharp eyes, Hummer grew more and more nervous. He paled until he was almost as clear as a jellyfish.

"Why, look at how he can change color! What clever camouflage you have, my friend! And these unusual fins—"

Dr. Puffer reached out to touch one. At the same time Hummer shied away. The fin fell off and drifted to the museum floor. Dr. Puffer, startled, gulped and puffed up to twice his usual size.

"Good reef!" exclaimed Sebastian.

Hummer stared from the puffed-up Puffer to the surprised Sebastian. Terrified, the little fish took off.

"Just as I thought!" Sebastian cried. "That's no angelfish—it's the bracelet eater!" He spun

around to face Alana. "I want to know what's going on here, young lady!"

But Alana didn't answer. Instead, she took off after Hummer.

"I want to speak with you, Princess!" Sebastian shouted from behind her. "You have some explaining to do."

Alana ignored him and kept following Hummer. The fish was moving fast, but it was obvious that he didn't know how to get out of the museum. Alana realized that he would soon be cornered. She called to him frantically. As fast as she swam, she couldn't keep up with him.

He *has* grown strong in the past few days, she thought.

Then she thought about what would happen if Dr. Puffer and Sebastian caught up with Hummer. Dr. Puffer would certainly want to keep Hummer and study him. Soon everyone would hear about Hummer. Scientists would come from miles around to study him and ask him questions. Sebastian would want to write music with him. Thousands of merpeople would want to see him. Hummer would never be free again.

Ahead of Alana, the fish turned sharply to

the right, heading into the Mysteries of the Sea wing. "No, Hummer!" she cried desperately. "That's a dead end!"

But he didn't stop. As he disappeared around the corner, Alana saw that the rest of his angelfish fins had come off. When she rounded the corner herself, he was nowhere in sight.

Alana whirled around, confused. How could he have disappeared? The only other entrance to the room was an emergency exit to the outdoors, and it was much too heavy for Hummer to open by himself. Where could he have gone?

"Up here, Al," Hummer whispered. "Pretty lucky, huh?"

She stared at the exhibit before her—the Sea of Meramera exhibit. Then she looked up and couldn't help but smile. There was Hummer, floating in front of a model. Beneath him was a sign that read MYTHICAL HUMFISH.

Alana could hear Dr. Puffer and Sebastian coming down the hall. "Can you hold very still?" she asked Hummer.

"Just you watch," Hummer said.

A moment later Dr. Puffer burst into the room. Sebastian scuttled in behind him.

"Where is he?" Sebastian asked breathlessly.

Alana lifted her hands and shrugged. "He got away."

Sebastian looked suspicious. He turned and surveyed the room, his gaze lingering on the Meramera exhibit. Dr. Puffer studied it, too. Hummer held perfectly still.

"Well, Sebastian," Dr. Puffer said at last. "Our interesting little friend seems to have given us the slip. We may as well head back to the crustacean wing."

Sebastian turned to Alana, still out of breath. "I will want to speak with you back at the palace, young lady."

Alana nodded.

"You see how it is for me, Puff," Sebastian complained. "I try to educate young princesses, and I end up chasing fish!" The two friends drifted off down the hall.

When they had disappeared around a corner, Alana and Hummer looked at each other. "Whew!" they said at the same time. Then they laughed. Hummer swam down to her.

"I know you must like this exhibit," Alana said quietly.

Hummer did. He darted about, looking at the models of the mysterious creatures that lived in Meramera. He didn't say a word. He didn't have to. His melodious humming and the beautiful colors that flowed down his body spoke for him.

"Hummer," said Alana when he had returned to her, "it's time for you to go."

"OK," he said agreeably. "Let's go back to the palace."

"No, that's not quite what I meant," Alana said. She tried to keep her voice from shaking. "I mean it's time for you to go find your home in Meramera. I'm sorry I said you weren't ready before. I was wrong. I just didn't want you to leave."

Hummer brushed up against her, glowing a soft pale blue.

"You belong in Meramera," she went on. "And I know that even though it's a long and difficult journey, you'll make it there. You are more than beautiful, Hummer. You're strong and clever, too."

"You're strong and clever and beautiful, too, Al," Hummer said, the blue of his scales deepening. "And you're the best friend I'll ever have. I'll miss you."

Alana knew that if she said anything else she would start to cry. So instead, she gave her friend a big hug and then swam with him to the emergency exit. Together they managed to open the heavy door. "Go quickly," she told him.

Hummer swam through the door, then turned to gaze at her for a moment. "Thanks for everything, Al," he said. "Please tell your sisters I said good-bye."

"I will," she promised, stroking the scales on his head one last time.

"Maybe someday," he said, glowing a brilliant pink, "we'll see each other again." He turned to swim away. "I'll never forget you, Al!" he called back with a wave of one fin.

She watched him swim off. His scales changed from pink to violet to blue to green as he swam. "I'll never forget you, either," she whispered as he disappeared from sight.

Then Alana let the door fall shut and returned to the Meramera exhibit. She wanted to take one last look at the humfish model. She was startled to find Dr. Puffer waiting for her there.

"So," he said, "I see that I have to make the model a little larger, with a longer tail. But it was a good guess, wasn't it—considering that I had never seen a real humfish until now."

Alana gasped. "You—you knew?"

"Did you really think you could fool an old

74

sea puff like me?" he asked. "Besides, I sent Sebastian on ahead and came back to eavesdrop a bit."

Alana shook her head and smiled. But as she did, the tears she had been holding back began to fall.

"There, there," Dr. Puffer said kindly, laying a comforting fin on her shoulder. "You did the right thing, my dear, even though I know it was difficult for you to let him go." He chuckled. "Believe me, it was difficult for me to see him go, too. I would have liked an opportunity to speak with him and study him. But your friend has to be free to live his own life however he likes, even if it's different from what we would like. It's a hard lesson, but a valuable one for you to learn—for I know that you love sea creatures as much as I do."

"What should I tell Sebastian?" she asked, wiping away her tears. Dr. Puffer was making her feel better already. She knew that he was right. She *had* done the right thing—for Hummer.

"Let me handle Sebastian," Dr. Puffer replied. "I knew him in his soft-shell days."

"Thanks, Dr. Puffer," Alana said gratefully.

"By the way," the scientist added, "now that Oceanvironmental Week is over, I could really use a bright student like you to help me with my work. With your permission, I would like to speak to your father about it. You could help me here after school, and perhaps on your next vacation you could join me and my colleagues on an expedition. The sea is full of marvelous creatures, Princess."

"That sounds wonderful," Alana said softly.

"And who knows," Dr. Puffer added. "One day you and I might even make it to Meramera."

Alana swam home dreaming about that. She wasn't crying anymore, but she wasn't ready to smile yet. She took the long way back to the palace.

When she arrived, her father and sisters were at the palace gate seeing off the last of the guests. The sisters noticed immediately that Hummer wasn't with Alana. They looked at her curiously. When they saw her sad face, they figured out what must have happened.

"Is Hummer on his way to Meramera?" Attina asked gently while the King was talking to Count Halfshell.

Alana just nodded. She was afraid that if she spoke she would start to cry again. She would miss Hummer a lot; but at the same time she loved the thought that he was swimming, strong and free, toward his rightful home. And maybe Dr. Puffer was right—maybe someday Alana *would* visit Hummer there.

Meanwhile, Count Halfshell was climbing into his conch coach. "Good-bye, Triton, and thank you for your hospitality," he said.

"Aren't you forgetting something?" the King said.

"Am I?" Count Halfshell replied.

Then the palace door opened, and Countess Oystera rushed out, veils and scarves trailing behind her. Count Halfshell blinked. "Oh, of course," he said. "My wife."

"It would be a terrible thing," Triton said, "if you were to leave this gracious lady behind."

The princesses glanced at one another and stifled their giggles. Countess Oystera clambered into the coach and blew a kiss to the King. "Good-bye, my dear, dear, dearest friend, King Triton!" she cooed as the coach pulled away. "I'm already looking forward to next year!"

As soon as the coach was out of sight, the princesses all burst into laughter. "Oh, my dear, dear, dear, dear, *dearest* Father!" Andrina cried, flinging her arms around him. "Why don't you have Oceanvironmental Week *every* week?"

The King joined in the laughter. "Well, well,

my daughters," he said when they had quieted down again. "Oceanvironmental Week was a grand success, wasn't it? Although some of our more—er—enthusiastic guests did keep me quite busy. I hope you girls had fun—and I hope you learned something, too. It's good to take some time once in a while to really appreciate the beauty and harmony of nature."

Ariel glanced at her sisters mischievously. "Well, Daddy, I think it's safe to say we all learned a lot about harmony this week. Right, Alana?"

Alana winked at Ariel and smiled up at Triton. "More than you know, Father!"